HARRY & HOPPER

Margaret Wild   Freya Blackwood

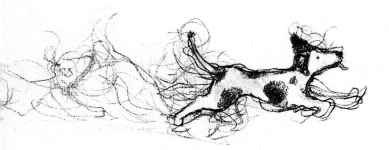

SCHOLASTIC

When the puppy came to live with Harry and Dad,
he was as jumpy as a grasshopper. So that's what
Harry called him. Hopper.

Harry taught him how to sit, how to stay, how to catch a ball,

how to fetch the lead, how to wrestle.

As Hopper grew older, he helped Harry with his homework, and Harry helped him run away from his weekly bath.

And every evening, Hopper sneaked past Dad to sleep on Harry's bed. He started at the bottom of the bed, then wriggled to the top, next to Harry.

"Goodnight, Hopper," said Harry. And they gazed at each other, their eyes gleaming with mischief and delight.

But one afternoon when Harry came home from school, there was no Hopper waiting by the gate. No glad yelping. No loving lick of the tongue.

Dad was hunched on the front steps. He said, "Come and sit next to me, Harry. There's something I have to tell you."

"Where's Hopper?" asked Harry, but somehow he already knew.

Dad wiped his eyes. "I'm very sorry, Harry. There was an accident. Hopper is dead."

"No!" said Harry.

He trudged into the house, dumped his bag, switched on the TV. He stared at the screen, but the words and pictures didn't make sense and he couldn't follow what was going on.

Dad asked, "Would you like to come and say goodbye to Hopper before I bury him?"

"No," said Harry, and he turned the TV up louder.

That night, Harry didn't want to sleep in his room.
Never again would Hopper wriggle from the
bottom of his bed to the top.

So Dad made up a bed on the sofa, and left
the small lamp on.

Harry lay curled up, longing for the feel
of Hopper, the smell of Hopper,
the bark of Hopper.

In the morning, Dad said, "If you like,
you can stay home from school today."

But Harry shook his head, and went to
school as usual. He didn't tell anyone —
not even his friends — about Hopper.

And again, he slept on the sofa.

In the middle of the night,
something woke him up.
He turned over — and there,
leaping at the window, was a
dog. A dog as jumpy as
a grasshopper!

Harry sprang off the sofa and
ran to the back door. He flung
it open.

"Hopper!" he cried. "You've
come back!"

Hopper jumped up and licked his ear. Harry hugged
the solid, warm little body.

The two of them played in the moonlit garden —
running, wrestling, shouting, barking.

When Harry woke up, he wondered if it had been a dream. He couldn't remember going back to bed, but he could still remember how alive and real Hopper had felt.

He couldn't wait for night to come.

And Hopper was there again, leaping at the window.
But he wasn't quite as solid, or quite as warm. Still, he
and Harry played with the ball and with sticks.

Harry told Dad about Hopper. He was afraid Dad
wouldn't believe him, but he just nodded and said,
"You can sleep on the sofa for as long as you like."

That night Harry sat up, waiting for Hopper.
But the window stayed blank and dark.
"Come on, Hopper," whispered Harry. "Come on!"
But Hopper didn't come.

Long after midnight, Harry
pushed aside the blanket and
went to open the back door.

There, curled under the
window, was Hopper.
As wispy as winter fog,
as cold as winter air.

Harry picked him up and took him into
the house, into his bedroom.

Hopper was too weak to wriggle from the
bottom of the bed to the top, so Harry
settled him on the pillow. Hopper's eyes
glimmered with mischief and delight.

The two of them lay close, heads together.

"Goodbye, Hopper," said Harry softly.